W9-BSO-541

3086 00374077 4

≠
Sal4fr

FRAN ELLEN'S HOUSE

ALSO BY MARILYN SACHS

FRAN ELLEN'S HOUSE

Marilyn Sachs

E. P. DUTTON   NEW YORK

Copyright © 1987 by Marilyn Sachs

All rights reserved. No part of this publication may be
reproduced or transmitted in any form or by any means,
electronic or mechanical, including photocopy, recording,
or any information storage and retrieval system now
known or to be invented, without permission in writing
from the publisher, except by a reviewer who wishes to
quote brief passages in connection with a review written
for inclusion in a magazine, newspaper, or broadcast.

Library of Congress Cataloging-in-Publication Data

Sachs, Marilyn.
    Fran Ellen's house.

    Summary: When Fran Ellen and her brother and
sisters reunite with their mother after living
with foster families for two years, Fran Ellen has a
difficult time adjusting to her new life.
    [1. Family life—Fiction.   2. Dollhouses—Fiction]
I. Title.
PZ7.S1187Fr 1987   [Fic] 87-19951
ISBN 0-525-44345-2

Published in the United States by E. P. Dutton,
2 Park Avenue, New York, N.Y. 10016,
a division of NAL Penguin Inc.

Published simultaneously in Canada by
Fitzhenry & Whiteside Limited, Toronto

Editor: Ann Durell   Designer: Barbara Powderly

Printed in the U.S.A.   W   First Edition
10 9 8 7 6 5 4 3 2 1

with love to Zack Rogow

August

Baby Bear is crying.

I pick him up and say, "Don't cry, Baby Bear. I've come back. For good. And now we are all together again."

He doesn't hear me.

"I want my mama," he says. "Where is my mama?"

I look around for her. She is lying facedown under the table in the kitchen. I pick her up and see that she has a deep crack on one side of her china head, and black smudges all over her face. She is mad, too. "Will you stop that yowling," she yells at Baby Bear. "Don't I have enough to do around this place without you caterwauling!"

"Don't worry, Mama Bear," I tell her. "Now that I'm back, we'll get everything shipshape in a jiffy."

She doesn't hear me either.

"I'm lonely," Baby Bear cries. "I don't have any-

body to play with. I want Goldilocks and I want Fran Ellen."

Mama Bear just about jumps out of my hand, she is so mad. "Don't you ever mention that person's name to me again," Mama Bear yells. "She is a liar and a traitor and a mean, no-good skunk. Didn't she promise she would take care of us? Didn't she say we'd always be together? Didn't she say not to worry, she'd be back soon, and in the meantime she'd make sure we were taken care of? And just look at the state we're in. Just look!"

"It wasn't my fault, Mama Bear," I whisper. "Please, Mama Bear, listen to me. It wasn't my fault."

"Fran Ellen, will you stop playing with that doll's house, and get in here and help." My mama is shouting.

I put Baby Bear and Mama Bear back in their house, and hurry into the kitchen. My mama is busy unpacking dishes, and Fletcher, my brother, is standing on a stepladder putting things away. Flora is sitting on the floor, crying.

"Will you get that child out of here," Mama says. "I asked Florence and Felice to look after her, but I don't know where they've gone to." Mama stamps her foot on the floor. "Another cockroach!"

Mama says. "Wherever you look in this place, you find cockroaches."

"Florence said she was going to take the garbage down," Fletcher says in his deep, manly voice which doesn't sound like him at all. "Maybe Felice went with her." I haven't seen him in over a year, and he has grown tall and has little hairs on his upper lip. It is embarrassing for me to look at those little hairs and to hear his new voice. Mama looks the same, only fatter and older.

"I want to go home," Flora sobs. She is three now, my beautiful baby sister, Flora. I haven't seen her either for more than a year, but she is still my beautiful Flora, who I love best in the world. She has soft, pale blonde curls all over her head, and big blue eyes, full up with tears now. "I want to go home," she keeps crying.

I pick her up and carry her into the bedroom she and I will share. "You are home, Flora. We are all home now."

"No, no, no!" she cries, wriggling in my arms like a slippery eel. "I want to go home!"

"Listen, Flora," I say, sitting down on one of the beds, and trying to rock her. She used to like when I rocked her. "You are home now with me. With Fran Ellen. And with Mama and Fletcher and Felice and Florence. This is home, now."

"No!" she says, pulling herself out of my arms and standing in front of me. She is looking at me like she doesn't know who I am and doesn't like what she sees. "I want to go home. I want Aunt Helen and Uncle Jeff and Susie and Bobbie. I want to go home."

I put an arm around her shoulders. "That was not your real home, Flora. That was a foster home because Mama was sick and Daddy—well, Daddy wasn't around. Nobody knows where Daddy went. So you had to go stay with the Carters."

"No!" Flora shakes her head, and all her little curls start bouncing around. "They are not the Carters. They are Aunt Helen and Uncle Jeff and Susie and Bobbie."

"Carter is their last name," I explain. "And Felice and Florence got to stay together at the McCabes', and Fletcher—first he went to the Franklins', and then later he went to the Petrinis'. And I—I went to three foster homes. . . ."

But she isn't listening. She keeps crying and saying she wants to go home. Finally, she lies down on her bed and falls asleep. She is only a little kid, I figure, and it won't take long before she gets used to us. She and I will have lots of good times together like we used to. She will get used to us, and she will love me best of all, the way she always did.

I go back into the kitchen.

Mama is sitting down at the table, one hand holding her head. Fletcher is still up on the ladder, but he is looking at Mama in a worried way.

"What's wrong, Mama?" he says. "Does something hurt you?"

"I have a headache," Mama says.

Fletcher comes down off the ladder. He goes over to Mama and puts a hand on her shoulder. "Did you take your pill, Mama?" he says.

My mama has to take a pill to keep her cheerful. If she doesn't take her pill, she will get sick and have to go back to the hospital again.

"Yes," Mama says, "I took it, but I still have a headache. Maybe it's because I didn't get any sleep last night."

"You're just tired, Mama," Fletcher says. "You go lie down, and Fran Ellen and I will finish putting things away."

"That's right, Mama," I chime in. "Fletcher and I will get everything shipshape in a jiffy."

Mama turns and looks at me. She nearly smiles, but then Florence and Felice come running into the room, all excited.

"Mama, Mama," Felice yells, "Florence and me went up and down in the elevator—"

"Did you take the garbage down?" Fletcher asks Florence.

"Of course I took the garbage down," Florence says. She is wearing lipstick and gook on her eyelashes, but she is the same Florence she always was—sneaky, selfish and mean.

"It certainly took you long enough," Fletcher says. "We've all been working hard here, and we need everybody to pitch in and not get lost."

"I came right back," Florence says, looking at me in an angry way. In the old days, whenever Fletcher told Florence off, she would pick on me.

"—and when we got downstairs," Felice was saying in her high, silly voice, "a boy told us somebody dropped a cat out of the window." Felice has always been fat and silly. She is seven now, and still fat and silly. "So we went outside, and there was this big crowd of people around the cat. Only he was dead. It was a black and white cat, and his eyes were bulging like this." Felice rolls her eyes around, and Mama gives a little sigh and rubs her head.

"Now you two just don't disappear," Fletcher says. "Mama is tired, and we are all going to pitch in and get this place in order. Florence, try to make yourself useful."

Florence stiffens up and shouts, "Well, I took the garbage down, and I only went along with Felice because I knew Mama would want me to keep an eye on her. But Fran Ellen's just standing around here, doing nothing. She always gets away with murder, and you never pick on her."

Then she reaches over and gives me a poke in my ribs like she always used to do. She probably figures I won't hit her back. I didn't used to in the old days. But I'm different now. So I just lean over and whack her one across her mean face. "Keep your hands to yourself," I say.

"You hit me!" Florence screams. "You hit me!"

"I sure did," I yell back. "And next time, I'll knock your teeth out. So you just better be careful."

"Mama! Mama!" Felice screams. "Fran Ellen hit Florence. Mama!"

Felice is screaming and Florence is screaming and I am screaming too.

Mama just kind of moans and puts her head in her hands. But Fletcher grabs Florence and me, and begins shaking us. He is really sore, and he is screaming louder than anybody else. "Cut it out!" he hollers. "Cut it out, both of you! And Felice, you shut up too! Just look how upset you're making Mama. What's the matter with you?" He goes right on shaking us as he talks. "Do you want us all to go back to . . ."

He doesn't finish his sentence. He doesn't have to. We all know what he means, and no, we don't want to go back. So we all shut up and get to work.

It doesn't take us long to put everything away. There isn't much to put away.

"Ms. Rutherford says she will get us some furniture next week," Mama says, looking in the empty room that will be the living room. It has a green carpet that covers the whole floor. The carpet is worn and dirty in the middle, and clean and bright around the edges.

"They must have put a couch over there," Fletcher says, "and maybe some other furniture around the other side."

"Maybe we should put our furniture in the middle where the carpet is dirty and worn," Felice says. "Because it looks much nicer around the sides."

Nobody answers Felice. She sure is silly.

"Well," Fletcher says, "at least we have beds, and a table and some chairs in the kitchen."

"My bed is lumpy," Florence says. "It sags in the middle. Fran Ellen has a much better bed than mine."

Fletcher gives her a dirty look, but Mama is feeling better now, and she says, "The important thing is that we are all together."

"Yes," I say. "That is the important thing." I don't say that Florence can have my bed, because it's in the same room with the bed Flora is sleeping in—the smallest bed of all. I don't want Florence to have my bed because then Mama might say she should share the room with Flora.

Flora wakes up and begins crying.

"Oh, that child," Mama says. "Doesn't she do anything else besides cry?"

"Don't worry, Mama," I say. "I'll go take care of her."

Flora is sitting up on her bed. She is crying, and one side of her face is red from sleeping on it.

"I want to go home," she says, putting her finger in her mouth.

"Hey, Flora," I say. "Just look here at my Bears'

House. It's going to be in this room—your room and mine. Just look at it. You and me, we're going to fix it up and make it beautiful again. Do you remember how it used to look?"

Flora keeps right on crying.

"No, I guess you don't," I say. I try to put my arms around her, but she pulls away from me and jams herself up against the wall, as far away from me as she can get.

"Well, it used to be the most beautiful doll's house in the world. My teacher, Miss Thompson, gave it to me back in the fourth grade."

It isn't the most beautiful doll's house in the world anymore. Somebody has broken down the wall between the kitchen and the living room. There are some pieces of the wall still up, with sharp, raggedy edges. And somebody has broken all the downstairs windows, and taken away the icebox with all the food in it. Somebody has swiped the sheets and blankets from the beds, and broken the little brass door knocker on the outside door. And the itty-bitty floor mat that used to say WEL-COME is gone. . . . Baby Bear is still crying, and I pick him up and hold him out to Flora.

"See, Flora," I tell her, "this is Baby Bear. He's just about your age. You can hold him if you like."

Flora doesn't want to hold Baby Bear. She just goes right on crying. After a while, Mama comes in and tries to cheer her up. Then Fletcher comes in, and Florence. But she doesn't stop. Only when Felice comes in, she stops.

Felice is eating an Oreo, and I think maybe Flora wants a cookie too. I run into the kitchen and bring her one. But she says no. She stops crying, though, and she gets off the bed and follows Felice into her room. She just sits there on the floor watching Felice and sucking her thumb.

Fletcher says maybe she feels good being with Felice, because Felice is the same age as Susie Carter, who is also kind of fat. It didn't used to be like that when we were all together, because Flora always loved me the best. Almost the first thing she said was "Fra Fra." That's me. Fran Ellen. And Felice was always mean to her. She's still mean.

"Mama, Mama," Felice says. "She keeps looking at me and following me around. Tell her to stop."

But Mama tells her to try and be nice to Flora. Then Mama and Fletcher go out to do the shopping. I don't know where Florence goes. Flora tags along after Felice. She doesn't want me to come. It will take awhile, I guess, for her to get used to me.

So I go into my bedroom and sit down on the floor in front of my Bears' House, and begin to get things organized.

Fran Ellen's House

Papa Bear is missing. He isn't in the house, and I go digging around in the shopping bag where Ms. Rutherford packed all the furniture and stuff back at the shelter. Sure enough, there he is down at the bottom with a little, torn, Hawaiian grass skirt wrapped around his middle. I pull it off him because he's a china doll like all the rest of them, and he has his clothes painted on him. I try not to laugh, because Papa Bear is very dignified, and I know he will be mad enough to bust that anybody could do anything like that to him.

I hurry up and bring him into the house and upstairs to where Mama Bear and Baby Bear are. He is so mad he can't even speak. But Mama Bear sure can.

"Well, it's about time!" she says to him. "Some father you are, disappearing like that when we needed you most."

"They put a grass skirt on me," Papa Bear howls.

"So you went to Hawaii," Mama Bear screams. "I wouldn't have believed it possible—even for somebody like you who always manages to make him-

self scarce when there's any work to be done. Just look at what's happened to us while you've been off carousing with who knows who, and having yourself one great old time."

Papa Bear just stands there speechless, so I speak up for him.

"No, no, Mama Bear. You got it all wrong. He was in a bag, and some of those kids at the shelter put a grass skirt on him. He couldn't help himself, Mama Bear. Just like me. I couldn't help myself either. None of the foster homes I got sent to let me bring you guys along. Ms. Feingold—she used to be the social worker—she said I should leave the house at the shelter. She said she'd take good care of you all. But she didn't. I guess she didn't stay long, because then there was Mr. Holland and then Mrs. Johnson and now Ms. Rutherford. So don't go blaming him, and don't go blaming me either."

She doesn't hear me. Sometimes, in the old days, they didn't always hear me right away either. Maybe I will have to get their place fixed up a little before they know I'm around.

"I don't have anybody to play with," Baby Bear yells. "I want Fran Ellen."

"Don't you dare mention her name again," Mama Bear says.

"That's right," Papa Bear sputters. *"From now on, she is Public Enemy Number 1, and I never want to hear her name mentioned in this house."*

"Aw, now, fellows," I say, *"just give me a chance to explain."*

Nobody hears me. I hate it when nobody hears me.

"Well, where's Goldilocks, then?" Baby Bear asks. *"I want to play with Goldilocks."*

"Where is that child?" Mama Bear says. *"She is another one who just wanders off first chance she gets. I'll give her a good talking to when I find her."*

"Goldilocks!" Papa Bear calls in his great big voice.

"Goldilocks!" Mama Bear says in her middle-sized voice.

"Goldilocks!" I say in my regular voice.

I go back and look in the shopping bag where I found Papa Bear. She is not there either. Only some pipe-cleaner chairs and a few cheapie, pink plastic doll's house dishes which I will throw out. That is not the kind of stuff my bears are used to.

Where can Goldilocks be? I pick up the house and look underneath it. She is nowhere. Goldilocks is gone. Some kid at the shelter must have swiped her. She was the prettiest one in the Bears' House, with her blonde painted head and little blue eyes that opened and closed.

I go back inside the house and break the bad news to them. "Goldilocks is gone!" I tell them, but they don't hear me.

"She'll come back," Papa Bear says to Mama Bear, and suddenly she is smiling at him. I guess she really likes him.

"Yes," she says, "I guess she will. The important thing is that we are all together again."

"That's right," says Papa Bear, "and we will fix this place up again as good as new."

"I'm hungry!" Baby Bear yells. "Let's eat."

We look around in the kitchen, but the icebox with all the food is gone. Used to be there were great things in that icebox—pies and turkey and a big cheese, and strawberry cake and corn on the cob. . . . There's nothing left.

"I want something to eat!" Baby Bear yells.

There is nothing in the shopping bag but Papa Bear's grass skirt, the pipe-cleaner furniture, and the cheapie little pink plastic dishes.

"I'm starving!" Baby Bear yells. "I could eat anything, I'm so hungry."

I have no choice. I tear the grass skirt into little pieces and put it down on the table in the kitchen. The red-and-white tablecloth is gone, and so are all the chairs. Mama Bear is looking around. She is opening the doors of the cupboard. "Where are all my dishes?" she says. "Where are my fancy china dishes and my beautiful glass goblets?" She almost looks like she's going to cry. "And where are the chairs?"

I can't help myself. For the time being, it is the best I can do. "Just be patient," I tell her as I arrange the pipe-cleaner chairs around the table and put the ugly little pink dishes on the table.

Mama Bear is not pleased with my arrangements, but she has a family to feed, so she divides the food up on the plates and calls them in to supper.

Baby Bear comes running in. He doesn't even notice the chair he's sitting in, but he does notice the food on his plate. "What's this stuff?" he yells. "It looks like grass to me."

Papa Bear makes a disgusted face. "Bears don't eat grass," he says. "And besides, this looks like something I have seen before that I hate."

"Well, you two just sit up straight and you eat every bite on your plate," says Mama Bear. "It may not be the tastiest food, but grass is healthy and

nourishing, with lots of vitamins, and you're lucky to have it. Just think of the starving people in Africa."

I'm getting pretty hungry myself, and I hear Mama and Fletcher bustling around in the kitchen. This will be the first meal we've all had together in over two years and two months. I hurry in to help.

September

This school is like all the others. Maybe even worse. The only class I might stay awake in is science. Not that I like science.

My teacher was supposed to be Mr. Goodman —an old guy who was hard of hearing. We had him for the first week. He was so boring, nobody listened. Nobody even acted like they were listening. There is this one crazy kid in my class, a little, skinny kid with eyes that kind of pop out. He sits behind me and he keeps jiggling around so much and kicking the back of my chair, I have to tell him to cut it out.

"Cut what out?" he says.

"Cut out kicking my chair," I tell him.

"Who's kicking your chair?" he says, acting surprised and opening his eyes very wide, and moving them all around. But I don't laugh.

18

"You just stop it!" I tell him and turn around again. All this is going on while Mr. Goodman is droning on and on about air or something else just as boring.

"What's your name?" the kid says into the back of my head. I don't bother turning around. I just shrug my shoulders.

"Anyway, I know it," he says. Big deal! I know his name too. It's Joseph Rupp.

"Your name's Fran Ellen Smith," he says, "and I know your brother, Skipper."

"I don't have a brother Skipper," I tell him, turning around and giving him a mean look. "And stop kicking my chair."

But one day when I come into the science class, Mr. Goodman isn't there. For about fifteen or twenty minutes, no teacher comes, and the crazy kid gets up in front of the class and says he thinks Mr. Goodman committed suicide.

"How?" somebody says.

"He jumped off a bridge," the kid says. And he climbs up on a desk, holds his nose, and jumps. Everybody laughs. Not me, though. I think he's a real jerk.

"Or maybe he shot himself," the kid says, getting up off the floor. He sticks a finger against his head like it's a gun, makes believe he's firing it, goes staggering around the room, and finally collapses on top of the teacher's desk just as the door opens and Mr. Raphael, the assistant principal, comes in.

"Joey Rupp," he says, looking at the kid, "what are you up to now?"

"Nothing, nothing," the kid says, acting innocent. "I was just coming up to sharpen my pencil, and I must have tripped."

"Oh," says Mr. Raphael, "that's very interesting, considering that the pencil sharpener is at the back of the room."

All the kids crack up. Even me. Joey Rupp hurries back to his seat.

"I'm sorry to tell you, class," Mr. Raphael says, "that Mr. Goodman was suddenly called home because his wife was ill. So you will use the rest of this period to study. And Joey Rupp, why don't you come with me down to the office. I have a few dozen pencils I'd like to have you sharpen."

The next day, there is a substitute teacher. Her name is Ms. Carpenter. She is very young and very nervous, and she tries to sound tough when she talks to us. But nobody is afraid of her. She has been with us for a week and a half now.

"Mr. Goodman isn't coming back this term," Joey Rupp whispers into the back of my head.

I don't bother to answer him, but he doesn't care. Nothing can stop him from rattling on and on.

"He and his wife are in jail. They were operating a big dope ring and they got busted."

"Joseph Rupp," Ms. Carpenter says, trying to look tough, "can you explain to the class the four layers of air?"

"No, Ms. Carpenter," Joey Rupp says, very politely, "I'm afraid I can't."

Mrs. Carter calls all the time. Sometimes I can get to the phone first and tell her nobody is home. But most of the time, somebody else gets to it before me.

"I don't think it's right," I say to my mother. "She's just making everything worse. Why can't she leave us alone?"

"She's a very nice lady," Mama says, "and she really cares for Flora. And you can see how much Flora cares for her."

"But it's not right to let Flora go there for the weekend. She's not going to want to come home. She'll never get used to us unless she forgets about them."

Mama is sitting on the brown couch in the living room. Now we have furniture in the living room. We have a brown couch that opens up at night into a bed for Fletcher, a shiny blue chair, and a coffee table that looks like lots of things were spilled on it that were not coffee. We also have a small TV set on a big table. Mama is watching a program on the TV set. There is a beautiful lady in the program in a tight, fancy dress. She is sipping something from a glass with ice in it and laughing up at a tall, handsome man. Mama begins laughing too.

"Mama," I say, "why can't she leave us alone?"

"Fran Ellen," Mama says, "why can't you leave me alone? You don't have to be with Flora all day long. You're in school now, so you don't have to put up with her whining. Maybe if you leave me alone, I can have a little peace and quiet myself this weekend." Mama goes back to watching her program.

After a while, I leave her and go into the kitchen. Fletcher is sitting at the kitchen table doing his homework. Now that school has started, Fletcher spends all of his free time doing his homework. He is very smart.

"Fletcher," I say, "I don't think it's right for Flora to go spend the weekend with the Carters. She's never going to get used to us unless she forgets about them."

"She *is* used to us," Fletcher says. "She's eating better now, and sleeping, and she likes to play with Felice when she comes home from school. She's only a little kid, and she's lived with the Carters most of her life. It would be cruel just to cut them off from her."

"It mixes her up," I tell him. "She thinks she has two families, and she likes them better than us." I don't say that she especially doesn't seem to like me. It's all their fault—the Carters. If they'd leave us alone, she'd get used to me.

Maybe Fletcher understands what I'm thinking, even if I don't say it. Because he lowers his voice and talks like he's sharing an important secret with somebody he trusts. With me. "You know, Fran Ellen, it's been hard on Mama—taking care of Flora. I know you keep trying to take her out when you're around, to give Mama a rest. And I try, too. But Flora usually wants to be with Felice, and then Felice starts carrying on too. It's hard on Mama. Now that I'm going to start working weekends at the Pizza Shack, I won't be around that much to help out. Mama needs a little time to herself. Maybe if Flora goes to the Carters from time to time, it will give Mama a chance to rest."

"I don't like it," I tell him. "I don't like it one bit."

Fletcher sighs. Then he picks up a book. "Just try to be a little patient, Fran Ellen," he says. "It will all work out."

I know it will all work out, if only the Carters would leave us alone. Everything is just fine except for them. I don't like having to share a room with Florence, but I tell myself that it will only be for a little while. Until Flora gets used to me again. Then she will want me back in her room instead of Felice.

I go into my room—the one Florence and I now share. She is sitting on my bed, putting red polish on her fingernails.

"Get off my bed," I tell her.

"Why should I?" she says.

"Because it's my bed," I say. "It could have been your bed, but you said it was lumpy, and you didn't want it. So why are you sitting on it, if it isn't your bed anymore?"

I know why she's sitting on it. Because her bed is a mess, with lots of her clothes lying all over it.

September

I make my bed every day, the way I learned when I stayed with the Manheimers—or maybe it was the Porters. Anyway, my bed is always neat, which is why she likes to sit on it.

"It's too crowded in this room," Florence says, putting up a hand and looking at the bright red nails on it. "Your silly doll's house takes up nearly all the room."

"Just don't you call it silly," I tell her.

"I'll call it whatever I like," she says. "And it *is* silly for a girl your age—twelve and a half—to still be playing with a silly old doll's house."

She sticks out her foot and acts like she means to kick it, but she doesn't. She knows very well what will happen to her if she does. She gets up slowly and moves over to her bed, where she sits down on top of a bunch of creased shirts. The slob! She begins polishing the nails on her other hand.

Florence is just about a year and a half older than me, but she acts like she's all grown up. Her birthday is on November 19, and she will be fourteen. Fletcher's birthday was back in June, when he turned fifteen. Felice will be eight in January, I will be thirteen in April, and Flora, my darling little sister, Flora, won't be four until next July.

Florence holds out her other hand. "What do you think of this color?" she asks.

I finish smoothing the wrinkles on my bed from

where Florence was sitting before I bother to turn around and look. "It's okay," I say.

"I have lipstick that matches," Florence says. "Do you want to see?"

I shrug my shoulders but she gets up and looks at herself in the mirror above the chest where we keep our clothes. She puts on the lipstick. Then she turns around and smiles at me.

"Well?" she says. "What do you think?" She puts up a hand and pats her hair. I guess she's kind of pretty, but I'm not going to tell her.

"It's okay," I say.

Then I sit down on the floor and look inside the Bears' House. The bears are all upstairs in bed. I haven't had much time for them since we moved here, what with trying to get Flora to like me and helping Mama look after the house, and going back to school. But I did fix up their beds. There was an old apron of Mama's with green and red flowers on it that was all ripped up. She said I could have it, and I made sheets and pillows and light summer blankets for them one day. I tried to get Flora to work with me, but she said no.

"I'm going to a party tonight," Florence says. "Brian will be there." She smiles at herself in the mirror. She's been smiling a lot these days. She has two girlfriends now—Carol and Joyce. Both of

26

them live here in this building. Carol is on the third floor and Joyce is on the sixth. We are on the fifth, so it would be easy for all of them to get together, but most of the time they stay in their own apartments and talk on the telephone. There is also a boy that Florence likes. His name is Brian, but he doesn't call. Florence would like him to call, and she spends a lot of time talking about him to her friends over the phone.

"You sure are one dopey girl," I tell her.

"You'll be the same way," she says to me, "when you grow up and stop playing with that dumb doll's house."

"Winter will be coming on soon," Mama Bear says. "We will need some warmer blankets on our beds, and we should get some new curtains up on those windows."

"I'm sick of staying in bed," Baby Bear says. "I want somebody to play with."

"I'm here," I tell him. "Play with me."

But he doesn't hear me. "I want Goldilocks," he says. "Where's Goldilocks?"

27

Flora has started wetting her pants. Every morning her bed is soaked, and Mama yells at her. Which is wrong. Flora is only a little kid, and she's not doing it on purpose.

Ms. Rutherford, the social worker, tries to tell her the same thing. They talk in the kitchen in low voices, but I know Ms. Rutherford is telling her just to be patient with Flora.

Then Ms. Rutherford asks us how we all are. "Just fine," I tell her. So does Fletcher. But Florence complains that she doesn't have enough decent clothes to wear to school, and Ms. Rutherford says she will see what she can do. Felice starts in whining about Flora. She tells Ms. Rutherford that Flora keeps following her around, and that Flora cries at night and wakes her up, and that Mama yells at her if she yells at Flora.

Ms. Rutherford keeps on smiling. She says we should all just try to be patient and that everything will work out fine. She says that Florence seems to be having a good time, except for not having enough clothes, and that Fletcher seems to be okay too. Which is true. Fletcher is okay. He likes his job at Pizza Shack, and lots of times he brings pizza home on the days he works. Especially if somebody calls in for a pizza and doesn't come to pick it up. He is also happy at school. Mama is proud of Fletcher. She says he will grow up to be somebody.

Even though I don't say anything to Ms. Rutherford, I'm not okay. Flora can't stand me, and nothing I do makes any difference. I thought maybe she would enjoy playing with the Bears' House, but she doesn't. She still pulls away from me whenever I try to touch her. She doesn't do it with Florence or Fletcher or Felice—only me.

"Mama Bear is ugly," Felice says. She is standing in the doorway of my room. "You should throw her out and get another one."

"Go away," I tell her.

I pick Mama Bear up and begin washing her off again with a washcloth. I've had to rub very hard, but most of the smudges are gone except for the one I'm working on today, a sticky one that's all over her neck. She looks better than when I got her back, but the crack is still there on one side of her face, cutting off a piece of her mouth.

"She looks weird," Felice says. "She looks like this girl in my class, Valerie Johnson, who has a big scar on her mouth, only it's in the middle, and she talks funny."

"Get lost," I tell her. But then I see Flora standing behind her.

"Come over here, Flora," I tell her. "Sit over here, next to me. You'll be able to see better if you come a little closer, and I'll let you wash Mama Bear's face if you do."

Flora shakes her head no. She puts her finger in her mouth with one hand, and with the other, she grabs hold of the bottom of Felice's shirt.

"Let go of me," Felice yells at her. "Stop holding on to my shirt."

Flora doesn't let go.

"Mama!" Felice yells. "Mama! Mama! Tell Flora to stop holding on to my shirt. She's pulling all my shirts out of shape. Mama!"

"Oh, stop that yelling!" I say. "Leave Mama alone, and stop being so mean to Flora!"

"Can I wash Mama Bear's face?" Felice asks.

So I let her come into my room and sit down next to me. Flora comes along too, holding on to Felice. If that's the only way that Flora will come into my room, then I'll have to put up with it.

I give Felice the washcloth, and she starts scrubbing away. Poor Mama Bear! She looks much worse than Papa Bear or Baby Bear. They were dirty too when I got them back, but they both cleaned up pretty good. Baby Bear's shirt is a little faded, and

Papa Bear has a few scratches on the back of his head, but otherwise the two of them don't look much different from the way they used to look.

"Where's Goldilocks?" Felice asks, still scrubbing away at Mama Bear's neck.

"Somebody swiped her," I say.

"She sure was pretty," Felice says. "I remember how she used to sleep in Baby Bear's bed on a little lacy pillow, and she had teeny tiny blue eyes that opened and closed."

I look at Felice. She's concentrating on Mama Bear. She's big for her age, and fat, and very silly. "Go on!" I say. "You don't remember Goldilocks. You don't remember things that happened yesterday. You don't remember where your house key is even when Mama hangs it around your neck."

Felice goes to elementary school, while I go to junior high school. Fletcher and Florence go to high school. So that's why Felice has to have a key, in case Mama is out shopping when she comes home from school. But lots of times she loses the key or forgets she's wearing it around her neck. Yesterday, when I came home from school, I found her crying outside our door. She had the key right around her neck, but she forgot it was there.

"I remember Goldilocks," she says, still working away on Mama Bear. "And I remember there used to be lots of furniture downstairs in the living room, and a big icebox with food in it in the kitchen. I remember. Yes, I do so remember."

She holds out Mama Bear to me, and I see that the black smudge on her neck is all gone now.

Another day when Flora is hanging on to her, Felice says, "You should get more furniture for the Bears' House."

"Thanks a lot," I tell her. I am busy pulling out all the pieces of broken glass from the downstairs windows, and taking down what's left of the wall between the kitchen and the living room.

"If you take down that wall," Felice says, "there won't be a kitchen and a living room anymore."

"You are so stupid," I tell her. "Of course there'll be a kitchen and a living room. Even without a wall, there is still a kitchen and a living room. But one day soon, I plan on putting up another wall."

"Yes," Felice says. "You have to have another wall. And you need to put glass in the windows.

And then you should paint the house, too. It sure looks bad. Maybe you could paint it red on the outside, and on the inside you could paint the kitchen yellow, the living room pink, and the bedroom—maybe you could paint the bedroom blue."

I don't bother answering her, but I move away a little bit. Felice spits when she talks.

"And you can paint the wall—you know, the one you're going to put up between the kitchen and the living room—you can paint it yellow on the kitchen side, and pink on the living room side."

"Can't you just shut up," I say. I pull out a big hunk of wood from the wall, and I get a splinter in my hand.

"And then you need to hang pictures on the wall, and over the fireplace too." She stops talking for a second. "Oh!" she says. "Where is the fireplace? There used to be a fireplace over here, and there was a picture over the fireplace."

I stop working on my splinter and look at her.

"It was a picture of a girl," she says. "I think maybe it was a picture of me."

She begins to smile at me, a big smile, showing where a couple of her teeth are missing on top. One of her teeth is missing down below, and I can see a little, white, ruffly edge of a new tooth breaking through.

"No, it was not a picture of you," I tell her. "Who would want to hang a picture of you over a fireplace? It was a picture of my teacher, Miss Thompson, when she was a girl. Her father made the house for her birthday. You sure are silly." But I am surprised that she remembers the fireplace and the picture of Miss Thompson that used to hang over it.

She's not listening to me. She's wiggling a loose tooth in her mouth with her tongue.

"Do you know what Melissa Morgan told me?" Felice says.

I concentrate on the splinter in my hand. It's not a very deep one, and if I can get a good hold on the end that's not under my skin, I should be able to get it out.

"Melissa says that if you put your old tooth under your pillow, the Tooth Fairy will come at night and take it away and leave you money."

"Will you stop it!" I tell her.

"I put my other teeth, the ones that fell out before, under my pillow, but nothing ever happened."

"Dummy!" I say. "There is no Tooth Fairy."

"Melissa says there is. But I always put those other teeth under my pillow, and nothing ever happened. Now this tooth is coming out. I guess I won't bother putting it under my pillow, though."

I pull the splinter out and lick the hurt place.

"I wish I could leave it under Melissa's pillow. Maybe that's what I need to do. Put it under somebody else's pillow."

There is no point in talking to her. She is too silly.

I can't believe my eyes when I see it.

There is a tooth under Baby Bear's pillow the next day.

"You've got to be crazy," I yell at Felice. "And you've also got to have a lot of nerve putting your yucky tooth in my Bears' House." I pull it out from underneath Baby Bear's pillow and throw it across the room.

Felice begins to cry. "I thought maybe the Tooth Fairy would find it if I put it under Baby Bear's pillow."

"You just keep your hands out of my Bears' House," I yell at her.

Felice is really blubbering. "Melissa gets a quarter every time she loses a tooth, and Lori Saunders says she gets half a dollar."

Then Flora starts crying too. She has a cold, and her nose is running. Big tears pop out of her eyes, and she yells, "I hate Fran Ellen! I hate Fran Ellen!"

Both of them are bawling, so I tell Felice to shut up, and then I try to wipe Flora's eyes and nose. But she pulls away from me and buries her face in Felice's side.

"She's wiping her nose all over me," Felice screams. "Tell her to stop wiping her nose all over me."

"Shh! Shh!" I say. "Both of you calm down."

Flora looks up at me. Her little face is wet from her eyes and her nose. "I like Felice's tooth," she says. "I love it."

"Okay, okay," I tell her. "I'll go find it. You can have it if you like it so much. Just stop crying."

I look around the room and find it underneath Florence's bed. It is a grimy-looking tooth because Felice doesn't brush her teeth very well. I wipe it off a little and hand it to Flora. She kisses it. Felice's yucky, grimy tooth she kisses, but she doesn't let me go near her.

Then she puts it in my Bears' House. Right in the middle of the living room floor.

Felice stops crying and starts laughing. "That's just stupid, Flora," she says. "You can't put a tooth in the middle of the bears' living room." She reaches out to take it away, but Flora lets out one big scream. "I like it there," Flora says. "I like that tooth there. It looks good there."

"Okay, Flora," I tell her. "If you like the tooth there in the living room, that's where it will stay." I am very happy I can finally do something she likes.

"What is this," Mama Bear says, *"sitting here in the middle of my living room floor?*

"I'm very sorry, Mama Bear," I say, "but you see, Felice's tooth fell out and Flora insists I leave it there."

She doesn't hear me. How long will it take before she does? How long before I can be a part of the family like I used to be?

Baby Bear comes in and walks around it.

"Did you drag this in here, Baby Bear?" Mama Bear says. Her speech is a little bit slurred, because a piece of her lip is gone. But I can understand what she is saying.

"You're always blaming me for everything," he yells.

I try again. "Listen to me!" But they don't hear me. The two of them just keep walking around that tooth, and you can see Mama Bear can't stand the sight of it.

But then Papa Bear comes in, looking real cheer-

ful. "It's all right," he says to Mama Bear. "I shot it, last time I was hunting. It is genuine ivory, out of the mouth of one of those big, fat, ugly monsters I protect you from."

"Oh!" says Baby Bear. "My Daddy is big and strong and brave."

Mama Bear is pleased. "Now we have a trophy," she says. "A real trophy. Maybe we will hang it on the wall once the wall gets put up, or maybe we can even hang it over the fireplace when we get a new one."

She makes a big fuss over Papa Bear, and I don't say anything. Even if they could hear me, I wouldn't want to give him away.

October

Except for Joey Rupp, nobody notices me much in the science class. There is a girl named Maria Hernandez, who reminds me of somebody I used to know back in Harlan, Alabama, where we used to live with my daddy. Before we moved up North, and he took off. There was this girl, Sylvie, and she used to be my friend. I was a little kid then, just about Felice's age, and Sylvie was the same. I think she was maybe a month older than me. Or maybe I was a month older than her.

That was a long time ago, and when I look at Maria Hernandez, I remember Sylvie, and I remember Harlan and some of the good times we used to have.

Mr. Goodman is not coming back. He and his wife have moved away to Florida, so Ms. Carpenter will be our science teacher for the rest of the term. Every day she brings in different things, like tropical fish, plants, and a model of the solar system which hangs down from the ceiling. All the planets are supposed to revolve around the sun, but some of them get stuck and just hang there. Ms. Carpenter keeps hoping she can get the kids in my class interested in science.

Yesterday she came in, all excited, with a sheep's eye, and told us she was going to dissect it and show us the different parts of the eye. But when she stepped out of the room for a couple of minutes, Joey Rupp swiped it off her desk and put it on Lisa Franklin's seat. Lisa was standing up and didn't see him do it. Later, when she sat down and all the kids except me began laughing, and she realized why they were laughing, she started screaming and chasing Joey Rupp all around the room. Then somebody else started throwing the eye around, and by the time Ms. Carpenter came back into the room, it was a real nuthouse.

She looked like she was going to cry. She just stood there and didn't say anything. So then Maria Hernandez went around the room telling everybody to shut up. She even found the eye and brought it up to Ms. Carpenter, but it was too smashed up to do anything with.

Later, after class, I heard Maria Hernandez talking to Joey Rupp in the hall. She didn't notice me listening.

"Why do you keep picking on her?" Maria asked him. "Why don't you just leave her alone?"

"I don't pick on her," Joey said.

"Yes, you do," Maria said. She was good and sore. They were walking in front of me, and I just slowed down so I wouldn't pass them. "You think you're so funny, but you're mean."

"I'm not mean," Joey said. You could see he didn't like having Maria tell him off. I don't think he's really mean. Just a little crazy. "Ms. Carpenter just doesn't know how to take a joke."

"You are mean, all right," Maria said, "and you're a bully, too. Just because you get all those other boneheads in the class to laugh doesn't make it okay." She stopped to face him and she began poking him with her finger. "You just leave her alone, do you hear? I'm telling you—stop it!"

I couldn't hear what he said, but today when Ms. Carpenter was talking about how she expected everybody in the class to do a science project, he didn't moan and groan like the rest of the kids.

Fran Ellen's House

I hate October. I didn't used to, but now I do. I will go on hating October as long as I live.

One day Ms. Rutherford comes and takes me out in her car. She has a clean, shiny one. It's blue on the outside, with cream-colored upholstery inside.

"We are going to the best hamburger place in the whole city," she says.

I just look out the window and think how much I hate her.

She acts like she doesn't know how much I hate her, and she keeps going on and on about how there is going to be some money for new clothes for all of us now, and she guesses I can go shopping whenever I like.

"I don't care about new clothes," I tell her. "You're mixing me up with Florence. She's the one who cares about clothes."

She stays pretty quiet until we get to the restaurant. It's a clean, shiny one with clean, shiny tables and chairs, and glasses of water with slices of lemon floating on top. She asks me if I'd like a hamburger or a cheeseburger. I tell her I don't want anything.

But she orders two hamburgers. Medium. And some fries. And two Cokes. Then she takes a deep breath and begins.

"Listen, Fran Ellen," she says. "You're not a kid anymore, and I'm going to be honest with you."

I look down at the napkin under my fork. It's a red one with the name of the restaurant on it. Sloppy Joe's, it says. That is one crazy name for a restaurant, I think. Who would want to eat in a place called Sloppy Joe's?

"Your mother is trying very hard to get back on her feet again," Ms. Rutherford says. Then she goes on and on, talking about how Flora is just too much for her to handle. How it just isn't working out, that Flora is not adjusting well at all, and that Mrs. Carter really loves Flora and will take wonderful care of her.

"I love her too," I say, still looking at that napkin. "I love her better than Mrs. Carter."

Ms. Rutherford reaches over and puts her hand on mine. I pull my hand away. Then she says, "I know you love her, and I know you're feeling bad right now. But the person we have to think of most of all is Flora. And Fran Ellen, if you really love her, you'll want the best for her. You'll want her to be happy. And she's most happy when she's with the Carters."

"No!" I say. "No! She just goes there too much. She spends too much time there. You shouldn't let her go there so often. Let her stay home with us. You'll see. She'll be just as happy with us."

"Your mother thinks it would be best for Flora if she went back to the Carters," Ms. Rutherford says. "Your mother thinks it would be best for all of you if Flora went back to the Carters. After a while, of course, you can all go visit her, and maybe she'll come and spend a little time with you when she's older. But for the time being . . ."

She goes on and on. I don't listen. Then the hamburgers come. Ms. Rutherford says I should eat mine or it will get cold, but I just go right on looking at the red napkin that says Sloppy Joe's. After a while, I see that it's getting wet.

"You can take your hamburger home in a doggie bag," Ms. Rutherford says. "Maybe you'll be hungry for it later."

Later I'm not hungry for it, but Felice is. She eats it up and says it was the best hamburger she ever ate in her whole life. Even if it was cold.

Everybody tries to be nice to me—even Florence. She offers to put polish on my fingernails, and she stops sitting on my bed. Mama cooks all the things I generally like to eat—ravioli and fried chicken and chocolate chip cookies.

One day she calls me into her bedroom. Now she is sleeping in the same room with Felice, and Fletcher is sleeping in what used to be her room. He doesn't have to sleep on the couch anymore.

"I was thinking, Fran Ellen," she says in a kind of sweet, cheery voice. Maybe she's smiling. I don't know because I'm looking at the floor. "This is such a nice, sunny room. It's bigger than either of the other two bedrooms, and I was thinking maybe you'd like to move back in here with Felice."

"No," I say to the floor, "I don't want to move back in here."

"Well," Mama says, "you could move your doll's house back, and you'd have more room. I know Felice would enjoy having the doll's house here and . . ."

"Felice is a fat slob," I say. "All she does is whine

and complain. If she had been nicer to Flora, Flora wouldn't have wanted to go away. It's all Felice's fault. I hate her. I'm never going to speak to her again as long as I live."

Mama pulls me over to her and tries to get me to lay my head on her shoulder. But I stand there stiff. She starts patting my back, but I don't loosen up. "Felice is seven years old," Mama says. "She's only a little kid."

"I don't want to move back in here," I tell her.

She goes on patting my back, but after a while she lets me go.

Florence is in our bedroom with her friend Carol. I can hear them giggling, so I'm not going in there. Felice is in the living room watching TV. I'm certainly not going in there.

I go in the kitchen, sit down at the table, and think what to do next. There's nothing I want to do. There is a cockroach crawling along the wall. He doesn't seem to know where he wants to go. First he moves along the wall sideways. Then, all of a sudden, he stops, turns around, and goes the other way. But no, that's not right, either. Finally he just stays put, right where he is. He doesn't move at all. Just like me, sitting at the kitchen table, watching him and thinking how much the two of us have in common.

"Enough is enough!" Mama says.

"I won't!" I tell her.

"Oh yes you will!" Mama says. She puts her face up close to mine and grabs my shoulders. "You have been moping around here for nearly a whole month, and making the rest of us miserable just looking at your long face."

Mama stops talking for a second and gives me a little shake.

"You have also not been doing your share of the work," Mama continues. "Fran Ellen, I want you to look at me when I talk to you."

I look up into Mama's face.

"Okay. Now, I am busy day and night cleaning this place and shopping and cooking and trying to get rid of the cockroaches. Are you listening, Fran Ellen?"

"Yes," I tell her.

"Yes what?"

"Yes, ma'am."

"That's better." Mama tilts her head to one side to get a better look at me. "You need a haircut, Fran Ellen," she says. "And so does Felice. She also needs a warm jacket. It will be winter before you know it. Now, today is Friday. Tomorrow, I want you and Felice to go to the barber and get haircuts. Then I want you to go shopping with her for a jacket."

"Why can't Florence go with her?" I say.

"Because I'm asking you," Mama answers.

"No," I say. "I won't!"

Mama's fingers tighten on my shoulders. "Grief can make a person sick," Mama says. "Like it made me sick when your father walked out on us. It can also make a person selfish, because you forget about everybody else. There is a lot of work around this place, and everybody's got to pitch in. Including you. Are you listening, Fran Ellen?"

"Yes," I say.

"Yes what?"

"Yes, ma'am," I tell her. "I'm listening."

I go back into my room and close the door. I would really like to slam it, but I know Mama won't stand for it. Not today. I lie down on the bed and feel the anger rising up in my throat. Mama must really hate me if she makes me take Felice shopping. She knows how I feel about Felice.

I am too angry to stay lying down on my bed, so I sit up and think what to do next. I haven't been doing much all month. I look around the room, and

my eyes settle on the Bears' House. It's been a
while since I've even thought about the Bears'
House.

I bend down and look inside. They are in the
kitchen, sitting in the pipe-cleaner chairs around
the table.

*Baby Bear says, "I'm tired of sitting. I want to
play with somebody. Where's Goldilocks?"*

*"Stop talking about Goldilocks," Mama Bear
says. "She is not coming back. You will have to
learn to play by yourself."*

I don't even try to talk to them anymore. They
don't hear me. What's the good of having them if
they don't hear me? All the time I was away in the
foster homes, I kept thinking about the Bears'
House. About how it would all be the same once
we were together again. But it isn't the same. And
I don't mean because most of the furniture is gone
and Goldilocks is gone, and everything looks old
and shabby, but because they are angry at me and
won't let me in.

Something has changed inside the Bears' House.
Somebody has been doing things, and it wasn't me.
Somebody has broken a toothbrush and laid the
bristly end on the kitchen floor, and somebody has

stuck a piece of sponge on a lollipop stick and leaned it against the kitchen wall. Somebody has also put what looks like the top from a pen on the floor, and somebody . . .

I pick Baby Bear up out of his seat. Somebody has wrapped Baby Bear in what looks like the finger off a glove.

I open up the door of my room. "Felice!" I yell. "Felice!"

She comes, smiling, into my room. "Did you see what I did?" she says. "I was waiting for you to see."

"You've got some nerve," I tell her. "Who said you could put things in my house?"

"My teacher read us a story about doll's house people who eat off of buttons," Felice says. "But it was my idea to make the scrubbing brush out of Flora's old toothbrush, and the mop out of a lollipop stick and a piece of sponge. I also got the idea to make a bucket out of the top of one of Fletcher's marking pens. If you like, we could even put a little water in it so Mama Bear could scrub the kitchen floor. It sure needs it."

"Don't you dare put water in my house. . . ."

"And I thought Baby Bear looked cold, so I cut off a finger on my glove—I lost the other one anyway, and look how cute he is, Fran Ellen. And see how nice the table looks with their new dishes."

I want to tell her to stay out of my house, period, and out of my room, but first I take a quick look where she is pointing. On the table are three little buttons holding grains of rice and some dried beans.

"The bears got tired of eating grass," Felice says. "Don't you think they like the rice and beans better, Fran Ellen?"

I tell her to stay out of my house and out of my room. After she goes, I take another look inside the Bears' House.

"I think these new dishes are very attractive," Mama Bear says.

"I like the rice and beans, too," Baby Bear says.

"It's a lot better than eating grass," says Papa Bear.

Felice is mad because the barber cut off so much of her hair that she looks like a boy. She says the kids in her class will make fun of her, and she makes blubbering noises with her mouth.

"Oh, shut up," I tell her. "It will grow back again soon."

We are sitting on the subway, on the way to the store where Mama says we should buy Felice a warm jacket.

"Tell me about Goldilocks," Felice says.

"There's nothing to tell," I say. "Somebody swiped her, and she's gone. That's all."

"You have to get her back," Felice says. "You can't have the three bears without Goldilocks."

I don't bother answering. Felice gets up and goes to the front of the train. We are in the first car, so she can look right into the tunnel and watch the lights change. When I was younger, I used to like to stand there too. Not anymore.

After a while she comes back, sits down again, and says, "Did you like her?"

"Did I like who?"

"Goldilocks."

"Well sure I liked her."

"So how come you don't find her and bring her back?"

"Because," I speak very clearly, "somebody swiped her, and I don't know where she is. If I don't know where she is, how can I find her and bring her back? And stop asking dumb questions!"

"I'm hungry," Felice says. "Are we going to buy lunch?"

"No," I tell her. "We're going to buy you a warm jacket, and then we're coming home. We don't have money for lunch."

We find the girls' department in the store, but all the jackets are tight on Felice. They are also expensive. They cost more than the money Mama gave me. Then I remember what Mrs. Porter used to do when she got money from the welfare lady to buy me a jacket. She would take me to the boys' department and buy me a jacket there. She told me it looked just the same as a girl's. But I knew it was cheaper.

"Come on," I say to Felice, who is snivelling again because we didn't buy her a jacket. "Stop fussing, and let's go to another department where they sell jackets." I don't say it's the boys' department, because I figure she'll begin crying over that.

"Okay, Fran Ellen," she says, cheering up.

We get on the escalator, but go up instead of down. That's why we get into trouble. Because we end up in the toy department instead of the boys' department.

"Oh, look," Felice yells. "Just look at that great big doll's house."

She pulls me over and keeps oohing and ahhing over it. "It's big," I admit, "but it's nothing special. My Bears' House was much more beautiful when I first got it. This one's just ordinary."

"Oh, but look, Fran Ellen, this one's got a bathroom with a pink tub and a pink sink with little lights over it, and a pink toilet that opens and shuts. Your Bears' House doesn't even have a bathroom."

"They didn't have bathrooms in those days," I tell her, but she doesn't stop.

"And see, Fran Ellen, it has a living room and a dining room downstairs, and a laundry room and a TV room and—oh, Fran Ellen, just look up here. There's a bedroom for the Mama and Papa with their own bathroom, and a room for the boy, and here's the girl's room. Oh, isn't it a beautiful room . . . ?"

I don't say anything, but I think it's beautiful, too. It has a canopy bed with red-and-white checked material and lots of ruffles, and a white, furry rug, and a white desk, and a little white dressing table with a mirror. And sitting in front of the mirror is . . .

"Goldilocks!" Felice screams. "It's Goldilocks!"

"Shh!" I tell her. "Stop shouting. It's not Goldilocks. Just because she has yellow hair doesn't make her Goldilocks."

"Oh, yes," Felice hollers, "it's Goldilocks!"

"Will you stop it!" I say, giving her a little poke. "Everybody's looking at us. I'm telling you it's not

Goldilocks. Goldilocks was a little china doll with hair painted on her head and eyes that opened and shut. This is just an ordinary little plastic doll with yellow yarn hair."

"Yes, girls, can I help you?" says one of those mean-looking salesladies.

"Yes, ma'am," says Felice. "Isn't that Goldilocks?"

The lady smiles a superior smile and says that the doll can be anybody we like, that it costs five dollars and ninety-five cents, and do we want to buy it?

"No, thank you, ma'am," I say. "We don't want to buy it."

"I do," Felice says. "I want to buy it. Instead of my jacket, I want Goldilocks."

"It's not Goldilocks," I tell her, trying to drag her off. "It's just an ordinary, ugly little doll, and we have to go find you a jacket."

She pulls away from me, and then when I try to grab her, I knock a few boxes off a shelf.

"Oh, I am sorry," I say. I bend down to pick them up, and the lady bends down, too.

"I'm really sorry, ma'am," I say. "She's a pain in the neck, but my mother made me go shopping with her to buy her a jacket."

"The girls' department is downstairs," she says,

taking the boxes from me. "And the escalator is right over there."

It's obvious she wants to get rid of us, but I feel I should explain. "We've been to the girls' department already, ma'am," I say in a low voice, "but she"—I motion with my head to Felice, who has her nose practically inside the doll's house—"she's too fat for most of the jackets. And besides, they're too expensive. So I thought maybe I should try the boys' department. Sometimes you can get a real good jacket much cheaper there, and . . ."

"The boys' department is downstairs, too," she says. I can see she's not particularly interested in what I'm telling her. So I grab Felice and pull her away. She comes along quietly and doesn't say a word while I am telling her off on the escalator. She doesn't even make a fuss when we get to the boys' department and I pick out a couple of boys' jackets for her to try on. One of them, a brown one, fits her okay. It's also cheaper than the others. It's not a nice-looking jacket, but she doesn't seem to mind.

"It will keep you warm this winter," I tell her, "and it's big enough so you can wear it next year."

"Okay, Fran Ellen," she says. I can see she's trying to be agreeable. Maybe, I think, she's worried I'll tell Mama what happened in the toy department. Maybe she thinks I'll even let her have it when we get outside the store.

"Listen, Felice," I say, "everything's okay now, and I have some money left over from paying for your jacket. There's a Chock Full O' Nuts down the block, I noticed near the train. So if you want a hot dog and an orange drink, you can have it."

"Okay, Fran Ellen."

"And if you want a doughnut, you can have a doughnut too."

"Okay, Fran Ellen."

The way she says it, I guess I should be suspicious, but I'm not. We go down the escalator, and out the door, and we hear running footsteps behind us, and before we can turn around, somebody grabs us both.

"Just you stop right there," she yells.

It's a big woman, and she pulls the two of us back into the store with her.

"What's going on?" I ask her.

She drags us into an elevator and up to the fourth floor. That's the floor with the toys, as I see when the elevator doors open. Then I understand what it's all about.

"I didn't break anything," I tell her as she pulls us along with her. "Those boxes didn't have anything breakable in them. There was just plastic doll's house furniture in those boxes. I didn't break anything."

She drags us into an office. There is a man sitting there behind a desk, and the saleslady with the mean smile is standing on one side of it.

"That's them," she says.

"Ask her," I say to the big woman, who is still holding on to us. "Ask her if I broke anything."

The man gets up from his desk and comes around the front. He leans back against it and looks at us like we're garbage. "Okay," he says, "you'd better hand it over or you'll be in even bigger trouble than you're already in."

"Hand over what?" I say. I can't figure out what he's talking about.

"It was the little one," says the big woman, who is still holding on to us. "I saw her put it in her pocket when the big one knocked those boxes off the shelf." She lets go of me, and then I hear Felice begin to holler. I look over, and see the woman reach into Felice's pants pocket and pull out the little doll's house doll with the yellow braids.

"I've had it," the man says, reaching for the phone on his desk. "These kids think they can just come in here and steal anything they like that isn't bolted down. I'm just sick and tired of having my stock disappear. These two are going to learn a lesson they won't forget in a hurry."

Felice is yelling so loud now, I bet they can hear her all over the store.

"Just a minute, mister," I say. "Please don't call anybody. Please!"

His hand is touching the phone. "Well?" he says.

I am trying very hard to think of something that will stop him from calling the cops. Because I know that's what he is going to do. He is going to call the cops, and then they will come and take us away. Or maybe they will just take Felice away. She is one dumb girl, but she is my sister, and I can't let them take her away.

"Please, mister," I say. "She's only a little kid. She's only seven."

"If she's only seven," he says, picking up the receiver, "and already she's stealing, I hate to think what she'll be doing at eight." He gives a little laugh, but it is not a pleasant one.

"Mister, mister," I say, "don't! It's not her fault."

"That's right," says the mean-looking saleslady. "You were in on it too, weren't you, knocking over those boxes, and telling me your mother sent you here to buy your sister a jacket."

"That's right," I yell. "I told her to do it. It was me. Not her."

The man begins to dial, and I start crying. Felice and me. We're making so much noise now, they can probably hear us out on the street.

"Harry," says the mean-looking saleslady, "just a minute, Harry. Put down the phone!"

The man puts down the phone and holds his hands over his ears. "Will you shut up, the two of you!"

I shut up, but Felice keeps on howling.

"Shut up, Felice," I say, and give her a little kick. Then she shuts up too.

The mean-looking saleslady is looking at the bag I'm still carrying.

"What's in that bag?" she asks.

"Oh, it's the jacket we bought for my sister. Like I told you, ma'am," I say. "We couldn't afford the ones in the girls' department, so we bought this one in the boys' department."

"Oh, yeah!" She doesn't believe me, and she makes me open the bag and show her the jacket. Then she looks at the sales slip.

"It's just like I said, ma'am. My mother told me to go shopping with her and buy her a jacket."

The mean-looking saleslady squints her eyes at me. "So maybe you were telling the truth," she says. "Maybe you didn't tell her to steal the doll. Maybe she did it all by herself. I did hear you tell her it was ugly. I bet it was her idea, and not yours, to steal the doll, wasn't it?"

"Oh no, ma'am," I say. "It was my idea. She didn't want to do it. She doesn't even know what she's doing most of the time. She's only seven, and she's not very bright, and she keeps losing everything. But maybe I can pay you for the doll. I mean, I don't even want that doll anyway, but I'll pay for it."

"I want it," Felice says. "I want it real bad."

"She doesn't know anything," I say. I put my hand in my jacket, and quickly pull out the money left from Felice's jacket. "Look, I can pay you two dollars and eighty-seven cents right now. And then, maybe I can bring the rest of the money tomorrow. Maybe my brother and other sister will have some money and . . ."

"Go home!" the mean-looking lady says. "And don't come back!"

"You'll be sorry if you do," says the man.

The big woman behind me just snorts.

"Oh no, ma'am," I say. "No, sir, we won't be coming back. Thank you. Thank you."

I grab Felice and drag her out of the office, and out of that store.

"You are one dumb, stupid girl," I shout at her as soon as we get outside. "You could have gotten in real trouble. If they called the police, we might be sitting in jail right now. I'm going to tell Mama when we get home, and she'll really give it to you. She'll . . ."

Felice reaches out and takes my hand. "Fran Ellen," she says, "I'm hungry."

November

Now Mama complains about all the missing things as well as the cockroaches.

"I know I had a spool of white thread and a spool of black and a spool of brown," Mama says, "and then I went out and bought three new spools, but now my thimble is gone."

"You better cut it out," I tell Felice.

On another day, Mama says, "The top on my eyedrops is missing. Did any of you kids see it?"

"I told you to stop," I say to Felice.

Then Florence starts in. "Where is the top of my nail polish remover?" she says. "I know I put it back on again, but now it's gone. Just like the top of my Bubbling Wine nail polish. And I'd like to know what happened to my matching tube of lipstick."

She doesn't say I took it, because I am no longer

sharing a room with her. She and Mama are now sharing a room, and Felice and I are together.

Fletcher says somebody has been taking off the tops of his marking pens, which he needs for the charts and graphs he makes for school.

"Enough is enough!" I tell Felice. "One of these days somebody will look inside the Bears' House, and then we both are going to get it."

She smiles her toothless smile and promises to stop. "But doesn't it look pretty now, Fran Ellen? Doesn't it?"

Yes, it does look pretty now. Not as pretty as it used to look, but a lot prettier than it looked when I got it back.

The kitchen looks the best. I told her not to, but Felice went ahead and unwound the thread from the three spools of thread in Mama's sewing box. Then she put the spools around the table, and now they have become stools for the three bears. I cut up some fancy green wrapping paper I found in a garbage can downstairs, and made a tablecloth and napkins. The cupboard that used to be in the kitchen is still there. It is still beautiful. All the little china dishes and little fancy glasses are gone from inside, but the cupboard is the same. Felice and I, we've been filling it up with button dishes and glasses made out of beads and marking pen tops.

They're not real glass like the old ones were, but they look pretty anyway.

So far, we have not put in a new icebox, but we will. Meantime the bears have lots of good food to eat on their table. They have a choice of rice and beans and dry spaghetti and celery top salad and Cheerio doughnuts and jelly beans and chewing gum.

We're not just working on the kitchen. Felice and I got this great idea for making a pair of standing living-room lamps out of the tops of Florence's nail polish bottles. I made a shade for one lamp from the top of Mama's eyedrop bottle, and one for the other from a little fluted paper I found in an empty box of chocolates down in the garbage can.

It is truly amazing, the kinds of things people throw out. Yesterday, I found a beautiful ring watch. The glass is broken and one of the hands is missing and it doesn't go. But it is very beautiful, painted red around the outside, with blue flowers and green leaves. Felice and I will make it into a wall clock for the bears and hang it up in the kitchen, after we figure out how to get the watch separated from the ring.

"Tell me about Goldilocks," Felice says. She is arranging some dried flowers in Mama's thimble. We've set it in a clay base so it stands straight. It will be a vase for the living room in the Bears' House.

"I told you about Goldilocks," I say. "Over and over again. You know everything there is to know about Goldilocks."

I am cutting up a torn straw hat that I found in the garbage can. It will make straw rugs for the living room and bedroom, and maybe a little doormat for outside the front door. Yesterday, I found many wonderful items in the garbage can—a lovely glass knob that we have turned into a coffee table in the living room, a kid's stained shirt with pretty buttons that had birds painted on them. They will make fancy dishes to put in the cupboard. The shirt also had shoulder pads that I will make chairs out of. I also found a brass Girl Scout pin with an eagle on it. It will make a beautiful door knocker once I polish it up.

"Did you hate her?" Felice says.

That's one question she has never asked me before. "Of course not," I tell her. "Why should I hate Goldilocks?"

"Because the bears liked her better," Felice says. She puts the vase in the living room, to one side of where the fireplace would be if it was still there.

"They never liked her better than me," I say. "They always liked me the best."

"So then why are they mad at you?" Felice says.

I keep on cutting. "They are mad at me because they think I deserted them. They think it's my fault their house was wrecked. That's why they won't talk to me anymore."

I smooth the piece I just cut out of the hat, and lay it down on the bedroom floor. We haven't started decorating the bedroom yet, so all I have to do is move the beds out of the way.

"There," I say, "how does it look now?"

"Nice," Felice says. "But I think the room would look nicer with a furry white rug, like the one we saw in that doll's house in the department store."

"Let's not talk about that doll's house," I say. "But one day, maybe we will have real rugs on the floor. There used to be a hooked rug made out of rags up here, and Baby Bear used to have a little patchwork quilt on his bed."

Felice comes over and puts her arms around my neck, and whispers in my ear, "I hate Goldilocks."

I give her a quick hug and push her away. "Now why should you hate Goldilocks all of a sudden?"

"Because she's the one who made all the trouble, and they blamed it on you."

"Felice," I say, "you're really not a bad kid, but you *are* kind of dumb. Didn't I tell you the kids in the shelter messed up the house? They were the ones who broke the windows and swiped some of the things. They even swiped Goldilocks. So how can you blame her?"

"It's her fault," Felice insists. "I hate her, and I'm glad she doesn't live here anymore."

"Mama," Florence yells. "I've found them. I know where all the missing things are."

Mama comes into our room, and she and Florence look over our shoulders into the Bears' House.

"There are my spools," Mama says, "and there's my thimble."

"And just look what they did with my nail-polish tops. Just look, Mama."

68

"Listen, Mama," I say, "I was going to tell you, but I thought you'd be mad."

"Of course I'm mad," Mama says. "I don't like having my things disappear."

"And just look, Mama," Florence says. "They made tables and wastepaper baskets out of all those missing marking-pen and medicine-tube tops."

Fletcher comes into the room. "What's going on here?" he says.

"We found the tops of your marking pens," Florence tells him. "They're drinking glasses now."

"What are you talking about?" Fletcher says. He bends down and looks over my shoulder, into the house. "Well," he says, "will you look at that."

"You could have asked me, Fran Ellen," Mama says. "I would have given you the spools once I was finished with them."

"The bears couldn't wait that long," Felice says. "They needed chairs to sit on around their kitchen table. You wouldn't like it if you didn't have a chair to sit on around your table."

"Don't you be fresh with me, Felice," Mama says.

"Oh, she didn't mean anything, Mama. She's only a little kid. I'm sorry, and so is Felice."

"Look, Mama," Florence says. "Look at the way they pasted those old stamps on buttons, and hung them up on the wall. It's kind of cute, isn't it?"

"It's their relatives," Felice says. "That one is their Aunt Harriet, and the other one is their Uncle Wayne."

Fletcher bursts out laughing. "You must be kidding," he says. "That one is Martha Washington, and the other is Thomas Edison."

Mama begins laughing too. "Well, it really does look cute in there." She gives a big sigh. "And I bet they don't have to worry about cockroaches."

Then we all are laughing. Even Florence. Maybe she's cheerful because today is her birthday, and Mama says she can invite her friends Carol and Joyce for dinner. Mama is making chicken and dumplings, which is Florence's favorite dish, and a chocolate cake for dessert.

"Look, Florence," Felice says, "the Bears are celebrating your birthday too."

Which is true. There is a black checker with pink clay frosting on the table for the chocolate cake, and Felice and I have just stuck a few pieces of birthday candles in the frosting.

"Now, if that isn't adorable," Mama says, "I don't know what is."

She kneels down and sticks her face real close to the Bears' House. "You know what you need in here?" Mama says.

"Lots of things," I say.

"You need curtains," Mama says. "You don't want the neighbors looking in."

"There's no glass in the windows, Mama," Felice tells her.

"All the more reason for curtains." Mama stands up. "If you promise never to take anything of mine that doesn't belong to you . . ."

"I promise," I say.

"Felice?" Mama looks at Felice.

"Do I have to?" Felice asks me.

"Yes," I tell her, "you have to."

"Okay, Fran Ellen," Felice says, "I promise."

"And I want you to apologize to Fletcher and Florence."

"It's okay, Mama," Fletcher says.

"No, it is not okay," Mama says. "I want them both to apologize. Go on, now."

"I'm sorry," I say. "I'm sorry, Fletcher. I'm sorry, Florence. I'm sorry, Mama."

"Felice?" Mama says.

"Me too," Felice says.

"Okay, then," says Mama, "I promise to make curtains for all the windows in the Bears' House when I get a chance. But now, I want Fran Ellen to come inside and set the table, and I want Felice to go wash her hands and face, and Fletcher, I need you to take down the cake plate in the closet, and Florence . . ."

"Today's my birthday," Florence says. "I shouldn't have to do anything on my birthday." She is still kneeling in front of the Bears' House, looking inside.

"That's right," Mama says. "Today is your birthday, so all you have to do is be happy."

"Oh, I am, I am," Florence says.

And she is. Especially when she opens her presents. Some earrings from Joyce, a picture frame from Carol, bedroom slippers from Mama, stationery from Fletcher, and three new bottles of nail polish from Felice and me.

December

Mama killing cockroaches in the middle of the night gives me the idea for my science project.

Mama is tearing around in her bathrobe, whacking away at them with a rolled-up newspaper while they go scurrying off across the walls in all directions.

"It's just disgusting," Mama says as she whacks away. "I never lived in a place like this. No matter what I do I can't get rid of them."

There is one cockroach really making tracks, outdistancing all the others. I watch him as Mama closes in on him and his buddies, and suddenly I am on his side.

Mama is gaining on him. She is bashing all the ones right behind him, and even though he is way out in front, all by himself, I know he is not going to get away.

"Hey, Mama," I yell, "there's a big bunch over the sink. Hurry, Mama, or they'll get away."

Mama turns, and he escapes into a crack in the wall.

Next day I go talk to Ms. Carpenter about my science project. All the other kids in my class have picked one, and she's been on my tail just like Mama was last night on the cockroaches'.

"Can I do a project on insects?" I ask her.

"Why yes, Fran Ellen," she says, surprised. Most of the kids are doing ones on subjects she suggested, like growing seeds or drawing the planets. I am probably the only one who came up with an idea on my own.

"I'll bring a couple in," I say. "In a jar."

"That will be just fine," Ms. Carpenter says. "And of course you would also want to give an oral report describing the insect, his habitat, his food, his reproductive habits. . . . What kind of an insect is it, anyway?"

"How long does the report have to be?" I ask her. "And should I go to the library to find some information?" I don't really want to answer her question, which is why I keep her busy answering my questions. I don't think she would be happy to have cockroaches in her classroom.

She isn't. I bring in two of them in an empty mayonnaise jar, with bits and pieces of spaghetti, carrots, and chocolate doughnuts to keep them happy.

"Cockroaches!" Ms. Carpenter says. "They're cockroaches."

"Yes, ma'am," I say. "I caught them last night in my kitchen. I could get some more if you want me to."

"No, Fran Ellen," Ms. Carpenter says. "Two cockroaches is two too many as far as I'm concerned."

"Tonight," I tell her, "I will start working on my report. It will take me some time to read those books I got out of the library."

"Well, bring in your report as soon as possible," Ms. Carpenter says. "Cockroaches are not my favorite creatures. I don't know why I had the idea you were going to study beetles or ants."

"Yes, ma'am," I tell her. "I'll get working on it right away."

Every day she asks me if I'm finished with my report, and every day I say soon. I'm in no hurry to do it because when I'm through, I know she'll want me to get rid of them. The kids in my class go "Yuck!" and grab their throats when they first see the cockroaches. But after a day or two, Joey

Rupp gives them names—Romeo and Juliet—and some of the other kids ask me if they can give them pieces of their lunches.

"Sure," I say. "Go right ahead."

Ms. Carpenter says after a week that she wants me to bring in my report the next day. She says I should read it to the class, and then I can get rid of the cockroaches.

I go home and read the books from the library. One of them says that cockroaches are disgusting insects that eat garbage and spread disease. The other book says that cockroaches are disgusting insects that eat garbage and, it is suspected, spread disease, but that it has never been proved that they do.

Now I begin to get interested. I read some more and then I write my report. It is three pages long. And when I get up in front of the class to read it the next day, I can see a couple of the kids acting like they are already asleep. Even before I begin.

I tell them that cockroaches are more than 350 million years old, that they were around when the dinosaurs lived and are tough little creatures that will probably be around for at least another 350 million years.

A bunch of the kids groan when I say that.

I tell them that cockroaches can be found all over the world, and eat everything. I describe the little egg sack the female carries, their life cycle, and a bunch of other things. Then I end by saying that cockroaches are blamed for spreading disease, but that nobody's ever proved that they do. And that I think it's a shame to go blaming them for troubles they might not even cause.

"Well," says Ms. Carpenter, "that certainly is a very interesting report, Fran Ellen, and a very original point of view."

She asks the kids if there are any questions or comments. Naturally, there are none, but when she says I can dispose of the cockroaches now that I have finished my report, I tell her I don't want to dispose of them.

"Can't they stay here, ma'am?" I ask. "They can't get out."

Then Joey Rupp says he thinks they should stay in the classroom too, and Maria Hernandez agrees. She says they're like mascots.

So Ms. Carpenter says okay, they can stay in the classroom, but that I will have to take care of them and make sure they don't get out. She also gives me an A on my report.

Fran Ellen's House

Now they sit in my bedroom—mine and Felice's—and talk about my Bears' House. Only nobody acts like it's my Bears' House.

"Look at this wallpaper, Mama," Florence says. "Don't you think it will look beautiful in the living room?"

"No," I say. "I don't want wallpaper in the Bears' House."

Mama is finishing the second pair of drapes, for the second window in the living room. There is one window on either side of where the fireplace used to be, and where it will be again when Fletcher surprises us for Christmas with a new one. Mama is sewing little pieces of lace on a beautiful strip of dark red velvet that was once a collar on an old winter coat. The other pair of drapes is already hanging on the other window, and they are so beautiful, they make everything else in the room look tacky.

"Don't worry about that," Mama says. "There will be a few surprises later on this month."

"Oh, yes," says Florence, "there certainly will be."

"Not wallpaper," I say. "I don't want wallpaper. I want to paint the house as soon as I can buy some paint. I want to paint it white on the outside with maroon trim, and I want all the rooms inside to be cream-colored. That's the way it used to look, and that's the way I want it to look again."

Mama has made a pair of curtains in the kitchen out of a handkerchief embroidered with red and blue flowers. Upstairs in the bedroom are the red-and-white checked curtains with ruffles that she made for each window, and she also made red-and-white quilts for Mama Bear and Papa Bear's beds.

"How about Baby Bear?" I ask. "It's winter now, and he only has that thin little blanket I made him from your old apron, and the finger off Felice's glove."

"I have something in mind for Baby Bear," Mama says.

"Joyce's Uncle Alan works in a wallpaper store," Florence says. "He can get lots of wallpaper samples for us. If you don't think this one goes with the drapes, Mama, I can ask Joyce to ask her uncle to bring us some others."

"Didn't you just hear what I was saying?" I tell her. "I said I don't want wallpaper in my Bears' House."

Fran Ellen's House

"It's not your Bears' House anymore," Florence
says. "Is it, Mama?"

Mama bites off a piece of thread and holds the
drapes up to the window in the living room. "Now,
doesn't that look nice?" Mama says. "If I do say so
myself, I think it looks just beautiful."

"No wallpaper!" I say to Florence.

Sometimes when I come into my bedroom and
only Felice is there, sitting in front of the Bears'
House, she will look up at me, kind of surprised,
like she doesn't know me at first. I think I know
what she is up to, and it makes me feel bad. But
only for a while. Felice is different now from the
way she used to be. She's still fat, and maybe she's
still silly too, but she's a good kid, and I guess I love
her the best in my family now. Now that Flora's
not here, I mean.

Sometimes she tells me the kids in her class pick
on her. She says they say she's fat, and sometimes
they hit her and make her cry.

"Who does it?" I ask her. "Just tell me who."

I get so mad when she tells me the kids pick on her, but what can I do? I can't go beating up little seven-year-olds just because they make Felice feel bad. I'd like to, but I can't. Besides, I go to a different school from Felice, and the worst kids don't live around here.

"You've got to stand up to them," I tell her. "You can't let them push you around."

"They're bigger than me," Felice says.

"Then keep away from them."

"I try, but they don't keep away from me."

"Then just run away if you see them coming after you."

"They can run faster than me."

"Listen, Felice," I tell her, "I used to be a coward too, just like you, so I know all about it. Before Mama got sick and had to go to the hospital, the kids used to pick on me too, and I never hit back. But you have to, Felice. You just have to. Don't ever let anybody get away with it."

"They'll hurt me, Fran Ellen," she says, snuggling up to me.

"No, they won't," I tell her. "Not after you hit them back. Then they'll leave you alone. Like they did with me. And then maybe they'll even make friends with you."

"I don't want any friends," Felice says.

"Of course you do," I tell her. "Everybody wants friends."

"You don't have any friends," she says.

"Well, sure I do," I say. "In school I have friends."

"I'd rather be here with you and our Bears' House," she says.

Our Bears' House? "No! No!" I want to yell at her. "It's not your Bears' House. It's mine. Only mine." But I don't. Because I remember how it used to be for me when I was a little, lonely kid, and everybody picked on me. How the only place I felt really safe was inside the Bears' House. How I could make believe I lived there, and that all the bears and Goldilocks were crazy about me and always there, waiting for me.

"Tell about how you used to play in the Bears' House," Felice says.

"You know all about that. I told you how Baby Bear and Goldilocks and I used to play together, and . . ."

"I hate Goldilocks," Felice says. "I never want her to live here again—never, never!"

"You don't have to worry about that," I tell her.

"Say how the bears gave you a birthday party when you were ten. Say how they brought you all those presents wrapped in fancy paper, and how Mama Bear made you a cake."

"I told you already. Lots and lots of times."

"But I want to hear it again, Fran Ellen. Go on. Say it."

By now she is sitting in my lap, and both of us are on the floor in front of the Bears' House. She is sucking on a Christmas candy, and I can smell the peppermint smell when she opens her mouth. She lost another tooth yesterday, and I told her to put it under her real pillow, and that I was pretty sure the Tooth Fairy would find it. I think she knows who the Tooth Fairy is now, but she acted happy and surprised when she found the quarter under her pillow this morning.

I let her sit in my lap and I tell her how much fun I used to have in the Bears' House, how Mama Bear used to cook up a storm for me, and how Papa Bear used to let me sit in his lap. A long time ago. Before they got mad at me.

"They're not mad at you anymore," Felice says, her head on my shoulder. "They say it was all Goldilocks' fault, and they're mad at her. They're not mad at you anymore, Fran Ellen. They love you."

"How do you know?" I ask her.

"I know," she says.

Ms. Carpenter is asking who will take the plants in her room home over the Christmas holiday.

"I will, Ms. Carpenter," I say. I want her to think I am very cooperative, because I know what will be coming up next.

Ms. Carpenter gives me the big snake plant to take home. Lisa Franklin takes a couple of small ones, and so does Dolores Aponte. Joey Rupp offers to take the tropical fish, but Ms. Carpenter says she will probably take them home herself. Then she looks at me. "Fran Ellen Smith," she says, "you will have to take our two friends in the *Blattella germanica* family home with you." That's what she calls Romeo and Juliet. It means German cockroaches.

"I can't, ma'am," I say. "My mother won't let me."

"Well then," says Ms. Carpenter, "you can leave them here, but I doubt if they'll be alive when we get back after the holidays."

"I'll take them," says Joey Rupp. "My father doesn't care what I have in my room as long as it doesn't make any noise. He works at night and sleeps during the day and probably won't even notice I have them."

"No, let me take them," says Maria Hernandez. "They're both getting so big now, I think they need a bigger jar. We've got plenty of big jars at home. I'll put them in a big jar and maybe line it with pieces of paper. I bet they'd like that."

A couple more kids offer to take them, and Ms. Carpenter laughs out loud. She says the *Blattella germanica* have been about the most popular creatures she's ever had in her room, and that she's amazed they've managed to live this long considering all the junk the kids keep giving them to eat. She says Joey Rupp can take them home since he offered first.

"Where do you live?" he asks me as we are going out the door. I am carrying the snake plant, and he has the jar with Romeo and Juliet.

I tell him where I live, and he says he is just about four blocks away, and that I can come and see the cockroaches during Christmas if I miss them.

"I don't think I will," I tell him. "I have their brothers and sisters all over the place to keep me company."

He laughs and so do I.

Fran Ellen's House

Florence made a little wreath with a bright red bow for the front door of the Bears' House. For inside, she made a Christmas tree out of a piece of pine branch, and she decorated it with tiny bits and pieces of jewelry. There is a little silver bird on the top and some gold fish over on one side and a red heart over on the other. Different colored chains loop in and out of the branches with bright bubbles of glass from old earrings and necklaces.

And she made a gold and crystal chandelier that hangs from the middle of the living room ceiling. There never used to be a chandelier in the Bears' House in the old days, but this one is so beautiful, it just about takes your breath away. It's so beautiful, I even tell Florence I think it's beautiful.

"It's the most beautiful chandelier I ever saw in my whole life," I tell her. "I never saw such a beautiful chandelier—ever!"

Florence is practically jumping up and down. "Oh, Fran Ellen," she says, "I could hardly wait for you to see it. Isn't it beautiful? And it's just an old earring of Joyce's sister, Shauna. She lost the other one, and she says she doesn't even know why she held on to this one. She's too small and dumpy to wear such big earrings anyway. But just look how it catches the light when it moves."

We are all in my bedroom now, on Christmas morning, bringing in our gifts to the bears.

Mama made a little patchwork quilt for Baby Bear. It's a pretty one, but not really as pretty as the old one. I don't tell Mama that, because she's so happy with the patchwork quilt. She keeps going on and on about how her Grandmother Carver and her Great-grandmother Harrison used to be famous for their quilting. And how she and her brother, Coleman, as well as their parents, each had a quilt of their own. And how she's going to write back home—she means to Harlan, Alabama—and see if her cousin, Marybelle, might know what happened to the quilts she left back there when we all moved up North. Maybe, Mama says, she might even get started making a new quilt. Maybe for Fletcher, since he's the oldest, and then, Mama says, she could make one for each of us.

Mama also made a round rag rug for the floor in the bears' bedroom. It looks a lot better than the straw rug I put down a few weeks back. She says she will make a bigger one for the living room when she gets a chance.

I knew Fletcher was going to make a fireplace, and he did. It's every bit as nice as the old one, and he is very happy that all of us are going ooh and ahh over it.

"It's just some old pebbles glued on a little matchbox," he says, acting like it's nothing special. But I know he's happy because his ears are growing pink. Fletcher's ears always grow pink when he's happy.

So anyway, I'm not surprised about the fireplace. But early this morning, Fletcher kicks Felice and me out of our room, and we don't know what he is up to. It takes him a couple of hours, and when we keep asking Mama what he is doing, she just tells us to be patient and wait and see.

Finally he opens the door and yells out, "Now you can come in!"

All of us do. Fletcher stands there looking at us—Felice and me—waiting. Felice sees it first. "Windows!" she cries out. "You put back the windows! Oh, Fletcher, I'm so happy the bears won't be cold anymore now."

I have made a new sofa for the Bears' House out of some pieces of sponges that I covered with a silky blue-and-green striped material from a tie I found in the garbage can. It looks good, and so do the two scatter rugs I made out of a fluffy white ear muff.

"Now close your eyes, Fran Ellen," Felice says,

giggling. "I've got to put something in the Bears' House, and I don't want you to see."

I close my eyes, and it takes quite a while, because Felice isn't able to do it by herself, and Florence says, "Wait, I'll help you."

And then Fletcher says, "No, it isn't straight." And while all this is going on, I've got to keep my eyes closed.

"Okay, Fran Ellen," Felice says. "Now you can open your eyes."

I do, and at first I don't see it.

Felice is disappointed. "I'll give you a hint," she says. "It's in the living room." So I look in the living room. I see the beautiful red velvet drapes, the new blue-and-green striped couch, the chandelier, the new rugs, the fireplace. . . . And then I see it.

"Felice," I say, "you did this? All by yourself?"

"It was my idea," Felice says, "but Mama helped a little."

"Only a little," Mama agrees.

My picture is now hanging over the fireplace. Felice says, "It's an old one, from when you were only nine. But Mama says we will be taking new pictures soon, and then we can put your new picture in over your old."

I stand there looking at it, and Felice says, "The frame is a wooden button Mama had in her button jar. Doesn't it look like a real picture frame, Fran Ellen? Doesn't it look nice?"

Yes, it does look nice, and finally I say so. I say it looks beautiful, and I give Felice a hug. But it makes me feel bad seeing my picture hanging over the fireplace, and I know why.

But I cheer up pretty quick because it's time to forget about the Bears' House and think about us. It is Christmas, and there are presents for all of us, too. We go into the living room and look under the tree. It's only a little one, but Mama says next year, for sure, we will have a bigger one. Mama says next year she expects to be working again and making good money.

Maybe she will be able to work as a waitress. There is a lady who lives upstairs, Mama says, who works at a fish restaurant and makes lots of money just in tips alone. After the holidays, Mama says, the lady is going to put in a good word for Mama, and maybe Mama will get a job there.

Fletcher says he hopes to work one night during the week at the Pizza Shack, as well as weekends, but Mama says she doesn't want him to spend so much time working that he neglects his homework. Mama says Fletcher will surely be going to college if he keeps on the way he is. She is very proud of Fletcher.

Florence says she can make money baby-sitting, and I say I can, too.

"No, Fran Ellen," Mama says. "I want you home looking after Felice. Especially if I start working. You're the only one who can keep her in line."

I'm happy to hear Mama say so. I have no problem keeping Felice in line, but it's nice that Mama thinks I'm so important.

The presents are piled up all around the tree. Fletcher gives all us kids gift certificates to the Pizza Shack, but Mama he gives a pair of leather gloves. Florence gives us all paperweights. Mine has a pair of skaters on a frozen lake, and Felice's has Santa and his reindeer. All of the paperweights start snowing when you turn them upside down.

"Just beautiful," Mama says, turning hers upside down. Hers has a big tree, and a bunch of little trees around it.

I give each of them a bar of fancy soap I bought at the dime store, and Felice has made different cards for each person. Mine says MERRY CHRIST-MAS, FRAN ELLEN in the middle of a drawing of a big Christmas tree with lots of red and blue balls hanging on it. Mama gives us all scarves and gloves.

"Try not to lose them," she says to Felice in a

stern voice. But she's not really mad. Not today. Today is Christmas.

After the presents, all of us pitch in to help Mama with the dinner.

"Next year," Mama says, "maybe we'll be able to afford a new set of dishes."

But nobody really minds that the dishes don't match. The food is so good. It is the best food I've had in years. Nobody can cook like my mama when she's feeling good. We have roast turkey with cornbread stuffing, sweet potatoes with marshmallows, cranberry sauce, mustard greens, and for dessert Mama has made two pies—pecan and apple. I have pieces of both.

Later, after I help Mama with the dishes, I go back into my bedroom. Felice is there, and this time I hear her whispering. She is whispering with the bears. Like I used to. But they don't hear me anymore, and now I don't hear them either. That's why I felt bad when I saw my picture hanging over the fireplace. It doesn't belong there because it isn't really my house anymore. One day, when I get a picture of Felice, I will take mine out and put hers in. It's her house now.

January

Romeo and Juliet have a big family now. Joey Rupp says that on December 31, there were only the two of them, but the next day, January 1, when he looked into the jar, there they all were. Lots and lots and lots of them, ready to greet the new year.

Enough of them, says Maria Hernandez, to name after each person in the class, including Ms. Carpenter.

She doesn't mind. She says she never thought her classroom would be famous for its collection of cockroaches, but she's glad the kids are interested in something. She keeps bringing in information about insects, and now we will all be going on a field trip to the Museum of Natural History to see the insect collection. I have never been there, but Maria Hernandez has, and she says they have a great lunchroom.

Maria brings in a gallon jar for the cockroaches,

and a few of us stay after school to help move them into their new home. I cut up pieces of newspaper for them, and Joey Rupp makes a lid out of a piece of wire mesh. It isn't easy moving a bunch of cockroaches without their making a break for it, and Ms. Carpenter gets a little cranky, and says if we don't stop clowning around she's going to flush all the cockroaches down the toilet. But she doesn't mean it. I think she's even beginning to get as interested in them as the rest of us.

After we finish, there are three of us—Joey Rupp, Maria Hernandez and me. It's raining when we come downstairs, and we stand in the doorway looking out. We're still feeling pretty good about moving the cockroaches, and nobody acts like they want to go home. Then Maria says why don't we all go home with her. She lives right around the corner, and we could look at some other big jars her mother has, or maybe we could even look at an empty fish tank that might make a future home if our cockroach family gets any bigger.

So we go to her house. Nobody is home. Both of her parents work, and so do her four brothers and sisters. She is the youngest. It's a very crowded house, with lots of furniture and interesting things to look at besides the jars and empty fish tank.

We drink milk and eat fig bars, and kind of kid around. Joey Rupp gets a little silly, and begins crawling around on the floor, wiggling his fingers over his head like they're antennas, and making believe he's a cockroach. Then the two of us do it, too. We are still crawling around and laughing when Maria's father comes home. She tries to explain to him what's so funny, but he doesn't get it.

So Joey and I get ready to leave. "Next time," I say to the two of them, "you can come over to my house."

"In the spring," Mama Bear says, "we will paint this place inside out."

"What color?" Baby Bear asks. He is eating a Cheerio doughnut, and watching the front door.

"I'm really not sure," Mama Bear says. "Fran Ellen likes white with maroon trim outside and cream color for all the rooms inside, but I'm sort of partial to red on the outside, and different colors inside."

"Me too," Papa Bear says. He puts down his newspaper, and also looks at the front door. "I prefer red, too. Maybe she will change her mind."

Fran Ellen's House

Mama Bear is looking at the front door too. "I think she will," Mama Bear says.

"She's late," Baby Bear yells, getting off his chair and heading for the door. "I can't wait for her to come and play with me."

"Will you get away from that door," Mama Bear says. "You know she's in school and can't come until she's finished. Now you just sit down at the table and finish your doughnut. And don't get any crumbs on the floor."

"Can I watch TV?" Baby Bear says. "Until she comes, I mean. I'd rather play with her than do anything else. I like her much better than I ever liked Goldilocks. I hate Goldilocks now."

"Yes, you can watch TV," Mama Bear says, "but don't put your feet up on the sofa."

Baby Bear goes into the living room, and turns on the new TV set.

Papa Bear chuckles. "That child!" he says. "He sure is excited about the new TV set."

"Yes indeed," Mama Bear says. "We certainly are very lucky to be able to afford all the beautiful new things we have now." She is still watching the door, and Papa Bear laughs. "You are as bad as Baby Bear," he says. "Don't worry. She'll be here soon. She never misses a day."

"That's right," Mama Bear says. "She is a won-

derful child, and she certainly brightens this place up."

I come through the door as she is talking. Baby Bear hears me, and he comes running in from the living room shouting, "She's here! She's here!"

"Hello everybody," I say as I come into the kitchen. It sure smells good in the kitchen. I know Mama Bear must be making something wonderful in her new oven just for me. Maybe coconut cookies or vanilla cupcakes.

They are all smiling at me. They love me so much, it makes me grin from ear to ear just looking at them standing there, looking at me like I'm the cat's meow.

"Hello, everybody," I say again. "I'm home."

"She's home!" Baby Bear keeps on yelling. "She's home. Felice is home."

About the Author

MARILYN SACHS has garnered both praise and awards for her sensitive, often witty portrayals of children and adolescents. *The Bears' House*, first published sixteen years ago to high acclaim, was a National Book Award nominee, a *New York Times* Outstanding Book of the Year and a *School Library Journal* Best Book of the Year.

Mrs. Sachs says, "Ever since the publication of *The Bears' House*, readers have been writing to me, asking what happened to Fran Ellen and her family. So I decided to write *Fran Ellen's House* and find out myself."

Marilyn Sachs's many other books for young people include *Class Pictures*, *The Fat Girl* and *Baby Sister*. She lives in San Francisco.